# THE LOOK COOKERS!

Written by Jim Malloy

Illustrated by Hannah Stephey

3 Dreams Creative Enterprises
New Fairfield, CT

Published 2015 by 3 Dreams Creative Enterprises, New Fairfield, CT.

ISBN 978-0-9906045-0-1

Printed in the United States of America
Signature Book Printing, www.sbpbooks.com

Dedicated to

Mary Jane Malloy

and

James H. Malloy, Jr.


(Mom & Dad/Gramma & Pop Pop)


For inspiring us to be fearless

as we chase our dreams.

Matthew was a normal boy
in every way but one.

**M**atthew was a secret agent!
But not just any secret agent...

**H**e was an *eye spy.*

Most people thought Matthew was shy. But they didn't know anything about being a spy.

And they didn't know **why** Matthew had invented eye-spying.

They didn't know about the **LOOK COOKERS!**
Look Cookers were everywhere.
There were many different kinds –
Matthew had a code name
for each one.

**A**nd all the Look Cookers used the dreaded *eye contact!*

Matthew didn't like eye contact.

When people looked at him, he imagined that they could see right through his eyeballs into his brain...

AND SEE WHAT HE KEPT IN THERE!

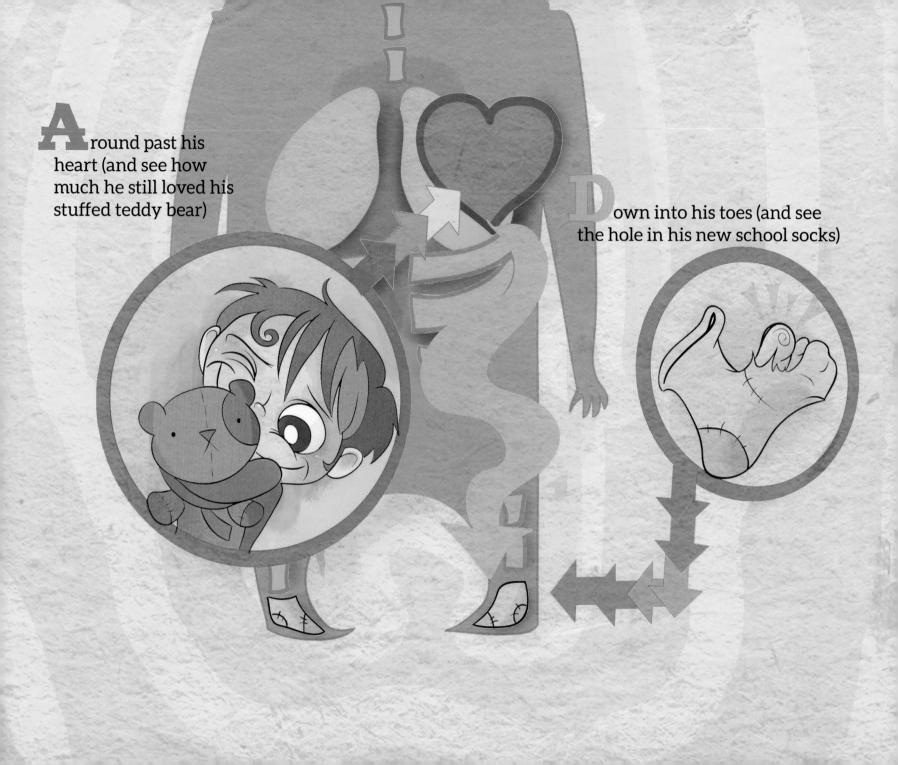

**A**round past his heart (and see how much he still loved his stuffed teddy bear)

**D**own into his toes (and see the hole in his new school socks)

They could probably even see the nametag his mother had sewn into his underwear.

**HOW EMBARRASSING!**

**O**n the morning of his first day of school, Matthew wasn't sure if he was ready for his most important mission as an eye spy.

The bus would be full of Look Cookers – ready to spring their *eye contact* on him!

Matthew stood with his mother at the bottom of their driveway as the long, yellow bus pulled up and stopped with a hiss.

"WELCOME ABOARD!"

said Mrs. Denton with a big smile.

Luckily for Matthew, Mrs. Denton was a *Glance Dancer* – a completely harmless Look Cooker.

*Glance Dancers* brush you gently with their eyes and then move on quickly to other things.

His mother gave him a hug. "Have fun, Matthew!" she said, with a tear in her eye.

It was time to go.

Matthew's heart beat faster with each step. And as soon as he got inside, he saw them!

There were at least thirty – squirming and jumping and making rude noises. It was going to take all of his secret agent skill to make it to the back of the bus – to an empty seat.

In the first row sat a pair
of twins: *Blink Drinkers!* Yikes!
Matthew was sure *Blink Drinkers*
read messages your eyelids sent
when you didn't even know it.

ACHOO!!

**H**e raced past them, watching his feet, trying not to scuff up his new school shoes.

Someone sneezed. Matthew looked up.

# oh no!

A *Gawk Stalker* in the second row stared right at him, wiping his face with the back of his hand.

*Gawk Stalkers* were nosy.

**"What's YOUR name?"** demanded the Gawk Stalker.

Matthew looked away, pretending he didn't hear the question.

Gawk Stalkers could also be annoying. They especially liked making fun of anyone wearing glasses. Luckily for Matthew, his eyesight was perfect.

"**Everybody take a seat,**" shouted Mrs. Denton, over the noise of the bus.

This mission was going to be tougher than Matthew imagined.

As he moved down the aisle, he dodged a *Peek Seeker* with large green eyes and a pretty blue dress,

scooted past a skinny *Stare Darer* kneeling on his seat, searching for a victim,

and barely made it through a bunch of *Gape Scrapers* who were wrestling for a spot by the window.

He glanced to the front of the bus to make sure no Look Cookers followed him.

*OK, all clear.*

**H**e turned around just in time to spot one of the most dreaded, **EYEBALL-BULGING, NIGHTMARE-IN-THE-MIDDLE-OF-THE-NIGHT** Look Cookers heading his way:

A SIGHT BITER! DOUBLE YIKES!

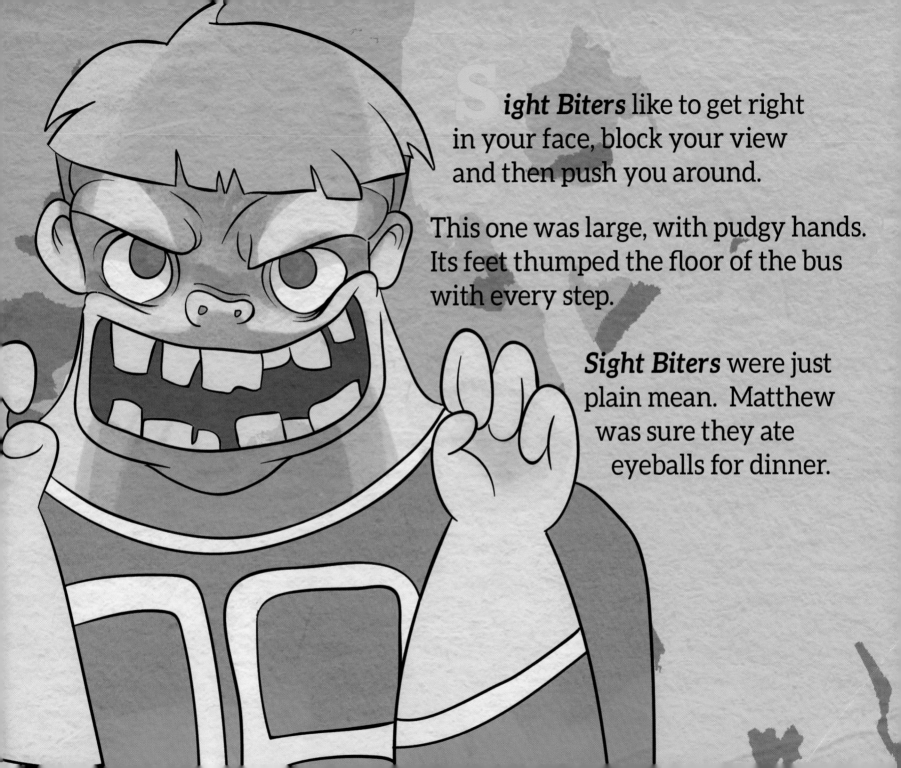

**Sight Biters** like to get right in your face, block your view and then push you around.

This one was large, with pudgy hands. Its feet thumped the floor of the bus with every step.

**Sight Biters** were just plain mean. Matthew was sure they ate eyeballs for dinner.

**HURRY**, he said. **THINK!**

An idea popped into his head.
Ducking down, he began to
tie his shoelaces.

The Sight Biter thundered by, calling out to the Stare Darer,

"HEY! GIT' OUTTA MY SEAT!"

Matthew slipped silently down the aisle.

*Whew! That was too close!*

Tested, but not broken – as they say in the spy game – Matthew finally found an empty seat.

It wasn't long before the bus pulled into the school parking lot. Outside the window, Matthew could see hundreds of Look Cookers waiting in line to go inside.

**M**atthew pulled his backpack over his shoulder. As he did, something fell out onto the seat. **Wow!** Matthew had forgotten about the **top-secret spy device** he had packed last night!

Now he was ready to complete his mission.

As he stepped off the bus and onto the sidewalk, Matthew overheard one of the other kids ask,

**"HEY, WHO'S THAT COOL KID WITH THE SHADES?"**

Matthew smiled. Today was going to be OK after all.